The Wacky, Wooly, Waba-Waba

SONICA ELLIS

DEDICATION:

This book is dedicated to my daughter Jada-Lee, who is my everything.

ACKNOWLEDGMENTS:

Thank you to all who helped me complete this, my second children's book!
My sincere gratitude to my illustrator, Harriet Rodis, whose art captured
perfectly what I had in mind.
Thank you to Piotr Grzegorzewski who graciously helped me
format the images and insert the text!
Special thanks to my editor, Jeff, who without my incessant nagging would
never have completed this :)

There once was a boy named Timmy,
and Timmy just could not seem to fall asleep.

Timmy tossed and Timmy turned.
Timmy fluffed his pillows.

Timmy even tried counting sheep,
But nothing seemed to work.

"Ugh," Timmy grumbled to himself,
"I wish I could fall asleep!"

As Timmy sat in bed wondering what else he could try, he heard a loud THUMP followed closely by the strangest voice he had ever heard coming from inside his closet.

"Oh Dear, am I lost again?
This simply will not do.
No no no. This will not do."

Timmy was a bit startled, but also very curious, so he got out of bed and walked over to his closet to take a look. Timmy opened his closet door slowly, creeeeak, poked his head in just enough to be able to see inside, and turned on the light...

Inside was the strangest thing he had ever seen!

In his closet, surrounded by his clothes and toys, was what looked like a giant panda bear!

Only this was not like any panda bear Timmy had ever seen. This one had fuzzy purple fur, big blue eyes, and little yellow wings!

It was wearing a giant red stocking cap and was pulling a big red wagon.

Upon seeing Timmy it spoke -

"Why, hello there! I am the Wacky Wooly Waba-Waba, at your service," said the strange creature bowing as he spoke.

Timmy wondered if he had finally fallen asleep and was dreaming. He rubbed his eyes and looked again.

"I understand someone here named Timmy is having trouble falling asleep. I am here to help!" said the Wacky Wooly Waba-Waba smiling.

"Do you know where I can find Timmy?" he asked fluttering his yellow wings.

"That's me. I'm Timmy,"

"Excellent!" exclaimed the Wacky Wooly Waba-Waba excitedly while doing a little dance. "Let's get right to it! But if you could first please help me pull my wagon out I would appreciate it so much Timmy. It appears to be stuck."

Timmy and the Wacky Wooly Waba-Waba pulled the wagon from under the toys out into the middle of Timmy's room.

"Thank you very much Timmy" said the Wacky Wooly Waba-Waba examining the wagon. "Everything seems to be in order."

"Now, are you ready for an adventure?" he continued.
Timmy nodded excitedly in agreement.

"Excellent! Hop in my magic wagon and let's go for
a ride!" replied Wacky Wooly Waba-Waba with a giant
grin and once more doing a little dance.

And with that the Wacky Wooly Waba-Waba hopped into the wagon
and took hold of the handle. "Next stop: Slumbertown and the
Pajamboree!" exclaimed the Wacky Wooly Waba-Waba, and with
a whoosh they flew out the window into the night sky.

Within a few minutes the two had landed in a small clearing. Timmy got out of the wagon and looked around. "Where are we?" he asked. "Why, we are here in Slumbertown for the Pajamboree", said the Wacky Wooly Waba-Waba.

Timmy looked again, "Slumbertown? Pajamboree? But this is just a clearing. No one is here but us" said Timmy a little confused. "Look again" said the Wacky Wooly Waba-Waba waving his hand.

When Timmy looked again he saw tables covered with all sorts of food and drink. Behind the tables was a stage. There were dozens of what looked like squirrels gathered in the clearing.

They were busy arranging the food on the tables, setting up chairs in front of the stage and even hanging decorations from the trees! Timmy saw one holding a banjo and another, a guitar. There was one with a harmonica, and even one with a fiddle!

PAJAMBORIE
PARTY

"Timmy," explained the Wacky Wooly Waba-Waba, "the people of Slumber
want to have a Pajamboree but they cannot find their pajamas!

You can't have a Pajamboree without pajamas! Would
you help them find their pajamas?" Timmy replied with
a smile "Of course!" "Excellent!" exclaimed the Wacky
Wooly Waba-Waba doing another dance.

Once all the pajamas were found and the squirrels had put them on, the Slumbertown Band began to play.

Everyone was eating and dancing and laughing. The fiddle player danced with the banjo player.

The harmonica player danced with the fiddle player.
And the Wacky Wooly Waba-Waba
danced with *everyone!*

After many songs, much eating, and even more
dancing, Timmy began to yawn.

"Ah, Timmy" said the Wacky Wooly Waba-Waba, "are
you getting sleepy?" Timmy nodded.
As much fun as he was having he had to admit he
was getting sleepy.

"Well, not to worry!
We will get you home and
into your bed lickety-split!"

And with a wave of his hand Slumbertown was gone as quickly as it
had appeared. "Climb back into my magic wagon and we'll head
home" said the Wacky Wooly Waba-Waba.

Timmy could barely keep his eyes open during the ride back, but before long they were back to his room.

The Wacky Wooly Waba-Waba helped Timmy out of the wagon and back into his bed.

"Wacky Wooly Waba-Waba?" said Timmy sleepily,
"What if I can't sleep tomorrow night?
Will you come back?"

The Wacky Wooly Waba-Waba smiled and said
"Don't worry about that Timmy. I have something that
will help," and he reached into his magic red wagon and
pulled out a tiny Wooly Waba-Waba.

"This is Wee Wooly Waba-Waba. Whenever you have trouble getting to sleep just rub his tummy three times and I'll be back!"

Timmy smiled, took the Wee Wooly Waba-Waba,
lay his head down, closed his eyes and said
"Goodnight Wacky Wooly Waba-Waba.

"Goodnight Timmy."

THE END

10142402R00018

Made in the USA
San Bernardino, CA
27 November 2018